☑ P9-CCU-565

CHARGE OF THE TRICERATOPS

DINOSAUR COVE™

CHARGE OF THE TRICERATOPS

BY
REX STONE

ILLUSTRATED BY
MIKE SPOOR

SCHOLASTIC INC.

New York Toronto London Auckland Sydney
Mexico City New Delhi Hong Kong Buenos Aires

**FOR JAMIE HEYWOOD AND TOM VOGLER
WHO HAVE ALWAYS LOVED DINOSAURS.**

**SPECIAL THANKS TO JAN BURCHETT
AND SARA VOGLER**

No part of this publication may be reproduced, stored in a retrieval system, or transmitted in any form or by any means, electronic, mechanical, photocopying, recording, or otherwise, without written permission of the publisher. For information regarding permission, write to Working Partners Ltd., Stanley House, St. Chad's Place, London WC1X 9HH, United Kingdom.

ISBN-13: 978-0-545-05378-5
ISBN-10: 0-545-05378-1

12 11 10 9 8 7   11 12 13/0

Printed in the U.S.A.
First printing, May 2008

FACT FILE

➡ JAMIE HAS JUST MOVED FROM THE CITY TO LIVE IN THE LIGHTHOUSE IN DINOSAUR COVE. JAMIE'S DAD IS OPENING A DINOSAUR MUSEUM ON THE BOTTOM FLOOR OF THE LIGHTHOUSE. WHEN JAMIE GOES HUNTING FOR FOSSILS IN THE CRUMBLING CLIFFS ON THE BEACH HE MEETS A LOCAL BOY, TOM, AND THE TWO DISCOVER AN AMAZING SECRET: A WORLD WITH REAL, LIVE DINOSAURS! BUT IT'S NOT ONLY DINOSAURS THAT INHABIT THIS PREHISTORIC WORLD. . . .

JAMIE

- FULL NAME: JAMIE MORGAN
- AGE: 8 YEARS
- SIZE: 1 JATOM*
- TOP SPEED: 7 MPH
- LIKES: FOSSIL HUNTING AND LEARNING ABOUT DINOSAURS
- DISLIKES: BEING STUCK INDOORS

Jamie's eye

Jamie's foot

Jamie's hand

*NOTE: A JATOM IS THE SIZE OF JAMIE OR TOM: 4 FT TALL AND 60 LB IN WEIGHT

TOM

- FULL NAME: THOMAS CLAY
- AGE: 8 YEARS
- SIZE: 1 JATOM*
- TOP SPEED: 7 MPH
- LIKES: TRACKING ANIMALS AND EXPLORING WILDLIFE
- DISLIKES: RAINY DAYS

Tom's eye   Tom's Hand

WANNA

- FULL NAME: WANNANOSAURUS
- AGE: 65 – 80 MILLION YEARS**
- SIZE: LESS THAN A JATOM*
- TOP SPEED: 31 MPH, ESPECIALLY WHEN BEING CHASED BY A T-REX
- LIKES: STINKY GINKGO FRUIT AND BANGING HIS HEAD ON TREE TRUNKS
- DISLIKES: SCARY DINOSAURS

Wanna's head   Wanna's foot

*NOTE: A JATOM IS THE SIZE OF JAMIE OR TOM: 4 FT TALL AND 60 LB IN WEIGHT
**NOTE: SCIENTISTS CALL THIS PERIOD THE LATE CRETACEOUS.

TRICERATOPS

Triceratops's frill

Triceratops's foot

Triceratops's mouth

Triceratops's horns

- FULL NAME: TRICERATOPS
- AGE: 65 – 80 MILLION YEARS**
- HEIGHT: 2 JATOMS*
- LENGTH: 6 JATOMS*
- WEIGHT: 280 JATOMS*
- HORNS: LENGTH OF A BROOM HANDLE
- TOP SPEED: NORMALLY SLOW,
  BUT UP TO 30 MPH WHEN CHARGING
- LIKES: BEING ONE OF THE HERD
- DISLIKES: BECOMING EXTINCT.
  IT WAS ONE OF THE LAST TO GO.

*NOTE: A JATOM IS THE SIZE OF JAMIE OR TOM: 4 FT TALL AND 60 LB IN WEIGHT
**NOTE: SCIENTISTS CALL THIS PERIOD THE LATE CRETACEOUS.

Landslips where
clay and fossils are

High tide beach line

Low tide beach line

Sea

DINO CAVE

Smugglers' Point

Jamie Morgan sprinted along the pebbly beach of Dinosaur Cove to meet his new best friend.

"Have you got everything?" asked Tom Clay, jumping off the rock he was standing on. "I brought my binoculars and my compass."

Jamie took off his backpack and rummaged inside for his fossil-hunting equipment. "I've got my pocket knife, my notebook, and the Fossil Finder." Jamie's brand-new hand-held computer had all sorts of prehistoric information at the touch of a few buttons. "I brought some sand-wiches, too," Jamie said. "Cheese and Grandpa's homemade pickles. It'll blow your head off!"

"I can't wait to get back to our cave," Tom said, hopping from one foot to another.

"You mean you can't wait to get back to the dinosaurs!" Jamie said, as the two friends hurried down the beach. Jamie had met Tom for the first time yesterday and together they had discovered Dinosaur Cove's biggest secret: an amazing world of living dinosaurs! First, Jamie had found a set of fossilized dino-saur footprints, and then the footprints had transported them to a place where dino-saurs still roamed the earth.

"It's hard keeping something so big a secret," Tom confessed. "My big brother kept asking me what I did yesterday."

"I know!" Jamie replied. "My dad got a huge triceratops skull fossil for the museum this morning, and I kept thinking about the *real* dinosaurs we saw yesterday."

Jamie and his dad had moved in with his grandpa in the old lighthouse on the cliffs, and Jamie's dad planned to open a dinosaur museum on the ground floor. Jamie's dad knew more about dinosaurs than anyone, but he didn't know the colors of a T-Rex like Jamie and Tom did!

"I forgot to tell you!" Jamie panted as they

scrambled up the steep path toward their secret cave. "I brought some colored pencils with me. I thought we could make a map of Dino World in my notebook."

"Good idea," Tom said. "We'll be like real explorers, charting unknown territories!"

"And seeing lots of dinosaurs!"

They reached the tall stack of boulders that led to their secret cave and climbed up using cracks in the rock. From the top of the boulders, Jamie could see his grandfather fishing out in the cove.

Jamie quickly slipped into the dark cave,

but Tom paused at the hidden entrance. "What if Dino World's not there?" he asked.

"What if we dreamt it?" Jamie laughed, and the sound echoed around the cave. "No way! That T-Rex we met was definitely real!" With a shiver of excitement he turned on his flashlight and shone it into the far corner. The small gap in the cave wall was clearly visible in the light of the beam.

Jamie took off his backpack and crawled through on his belly into the second chamber. It was narrower and pitch-black. Jamie and Tom suspected they were the only people ever to have been in this place.

Jamie aimed his flashlight toward the stone floor. "Here are the fossilized dinosaur footprints we found yesterday."

"The best fossil anyone has ever found!" Tom said. The footprints had somehow transported the boys to Dino World.

Tom stepped into the first clover-shaped indent in the cave floor. "Here goes!" He placed his foot carefully into each footprint, walking in the dinosaur tracks.

Jamie stuck close behind him and counted every step. "One . . . two . . . three . . . four . . . FIVE!"

In an instant, the cold, damp cave was gone, and Jamie and Tom were standing in a bright sunny cave and staring out at giant, sun-dappled trees. The air was hot and humid and they could hear the heavy drone of insects. They ran out onto the damp squelchy ground of Dino World.

"We're back in the jungle," said Jamie happily. "We're on Ginkgo Hill."

"This is so cool!" said Tom, looking around eagerly.

Jamie laughed. "Boiling, you mean!" He picked a large leaf off the ground and fanned himself. Suddenly, he stopped. "What was that?"

The boys listened hard. From somewhere in the steaming jungle they could hear scuffling—and it was getting nearer.

"Something's coming!" warned Tom.

Just then, a plump, scaly little creature with a flat, bony head burst out from a clump of ferns. It scuttled along on its stumpy hind legs and hurled itself at Jamie, knocking him flat on his back.

Grunk! Grunk! Grunk!

"It's Wanna!" exclaimed Tom in relief.

Jamie and Tom had met the wannanosaurus on their first visit to Dino World, and the Fossil Finder had said that it was pronounced "wan-na-no-saur-us." Wanna had helped when the T-Rex was after them and had turned out to be a true friend.

"Stop licking, Wanna!" panted Jamie, trying to push him off. "Your tongue's like sandpaper."

Tom reached up to a nearby ginkgo tree and picked a handful of the small, foul-smelling fruit. He held one out. "Have a stink-o bomb, Wanna. Your favorite!"

Wanna bounded over and greedily gobbled it up as Jamie staggered to his feet. Tom gave him one more and then quickly tossed a few more pieces of the fruit to Jamie, who hid them in his backpack.

"Let's start mapping!" said Tom.

Wanna sniffed the bag as Jamie dug around and pulled out his notebook and colored pencils. "We're here," he said, drawing Ginkgo Hill in the middle of the page. "Yesterday we found the ocean and the lagoon in the west." He sketched them in.

Tom checked the compass. "So let's head north today."

"Great," said Jamie. "Come on, Wanna! We're going exploring."

Wanna wagged his tail and trotted happily alongside the boys. They scrambled through ferns and vines and squelched among slimy giant toadstools.

At last they came to a break in the trees and peered through. Below was the dense tangle of the jungle and beyond that vast grassy plains with a wide river snaking through toward their hill.

"Look at those faraway mountains," said Tom, scanning the horizon with the binoculars.

"They're so high their peaks are
hidden in the clouds."

"Faraway Mountains—that's a
good name!" said Jamie, and he
scribbled it down on the map.

Then Jamie took the binoculars and scanned the plains, and

what he saw made him gasp. There were about fifteen strange-looking houses made of orange earth sitting near a curve in the river.

"What is it?" Tom asked.

"I don't know," Jamie replied. "I think...I think there's a village!"

CHAPTER 2

"No way!" Tom said. He grabbed the binoculars and gasped. "I thought we were the only people in Dino World."

"Me too," said Jamie. "But...who could they be? There weren't any people around during dinosaur times. Humans didn't come along for millions of years!"

"Well, if *we're* here," Tom reasoned, "maybe other people got through, too?"

"Or maybe the houses aren't for people at all, but something else," Jamie guessed, as he added this odd discovery to the map. "How should I label it?"

"I'm not sure," Tom admitted. "Since we don't know what they are, we need to investigate. That's what real explorers would do!"

Following Tom's compass, the two boys set off northeast down the rest of Ginkgo Hill. Wanna grunted excitedly as he clambered over roots and ferns. The trunks of giant trees rose into the misty canopy and insects as big and colorful as parrots buzzed around their heads. Soon they heard splashing and found themselves on the banks of a wide river that cut the forest in two.

"We'll have to swim it if we're going to get to those houses," Tom said, as he started down the bank.

"Wait!" warned Jamie, peeling off his backpack and pulling out his Fossil Finder. He flipped open the lid. On the screen a picture of a T-Rex footprint glowed and above it the words, **HAPPY HUNTING**. A cursor blinked at the bottom and Jamie tapped in the keywords: **PREHISTORIC RIVER CREATURES**.

"We might meet one of these," he said, handing the Fossil Finder to Tom. **CHAMPSOSAURUS**, read Tom. "Hmm. Looks like a crocodile."

"And we'd look like its dinner!" Jamie peered into the water for signs of life and spotted several grayish humps. "Look over there."

"Those are stones, fossil-brain,"

Tom said. "We can
cross there!"

When the three of them
reached the other side, Tom
checked his compass again and they
headed off through the trees.

"How long do you think it'll take us
to get to the houses?" Tom asked.

"Hard to tell," puffed Jamie. "But we've got to figure out what those things are for our map."

The boys stumbled into a large clearing surrounded by three walls of vines. Spiky plants grew all over the ground, and Wanna grabbed a clump in his mouth and chomped happily.

"OK, Wanna. Lunchtime!" declared Jamie. He climbed onto a log and tore the tinfoil off the cheese and pickle sandwiches. He was just handing a sandwich to Tom when Wanna leaped up and grabbed half of it in his mouth.

"Hey, that's my lunch!" exclaimed Tom. Wanna chewed greedily. Suddenly, the little dinosaur blinked in surprise and began to run around in circles, shaking his head and making strange *gak-gak* noises.

"He's discovered Grandpa's pickle!" Jamie laughed.

A deep rumbling sound from the forest made Jamie and Tom instantly stop laughing.

"Only something really big could make that noise," murmured Tom, glancing over his shoulder. "What if it's the T-Rex again?"

"Wait—I can hear mooing," said Jamie, puzzled. His attention was fixed on the wall

of vines nearest to
them.

"Like a herd of
giant cows," said
Tom.

There was a
sound of snapping
and splitting as the
vines just in front of
them began to shake.
Tom leaned forward
and Jamie dropped his
sandwich as the last
strands tore away.

A massive beaked
head with three
huge horns peered
into the clearing.

CHAPTER 3

"It's a triceratops!" whispered Jamie, transfixed by the giant head looming above him. "Awesome!"

Jamie and Tom could feel its hot breath on their faces. With a snort, the dinosaur forced its body through the vines and took a lumbering step into the clearing.

"I'm glad it's not a T-Rex," Tom said. "But I can't believe it's so gigantic!"

"Dad was telling me about triceratops this

morning," said Jamie. "They weigh about twelve hundred pounds—the same as an elephant!"

"I don't want that treading on my toes!" Tom hastily scrambled onto the log and pulled Jamie up behind him.

The vines shook again and another triceratops pushed its way into the clearing. Soon a whole herd of the three-horned creatures stomped into view.

One T-Tops put his head down to eat some of the spiky grass right in front of them. The herd munched on the grass, completely ignoring the boys.

"Look, Wanna!" Jamie said, as their dinosaur friend gobbled up a flower nearby. "They're herbivores, like you, which means they won't want to eat us."

"That's true, but if one steps on us, it would be just as dangerous!" replied Tom. "We'd better not risk trying to walk through them.

Maybe we should try to scare them away from the clearing?"

"I don't think scaring a herd of triceratops would be a good idea," Jamie said. "They might end up charging like a herd of elephants!"

They heard a lowing from the biggest dinosaur in the herd. The sound rumbled around the clearing as the others took up the call. It shook the boys on their log.

"The leader's given a signal," Tom said. "What does it mean?"

"I think it means they're moving on!" said Jamie. "And they're going in the direction of the houses."

The boys tried to keep their balance as their log was bumped from all sides by the tree trunk-size legs going by, but it was too much! Jamie slipped off the log and had to roll away quickly to avoid being trampled.

"What are we going to do?" Jamie asked, breathlessly, as he scrambled safely back onto the log. "We've got to get away from their feet!"

"It seems to me that the safest place is on top of a T-Tops!" Tom said. "Otherwise, we'll be squished!"

"Fossil-brain!" squeaked Jamie. "We would need a trampoline to get up there."

"Maybe we don't," Tom said. He pulled some ginkgoes out of Jamie's bag and held one out. One of the beasts stopped and sniffed the air. Then it turned its head to face the boys, and gave a blasting snort that nearly blew the boys off the log. Tom quickly dropped the ginkgoes onto the ground. The beast lowered its gigantic head and its frill was in their reach. Its powerful jaws ground noisily as it chewed the orange fruit.

Tom tossed several other ginkgoes onto the ground and whispered, "Now, we can try to climb onboard."

Tom quickly took hold of a horn and pulled himself up behind the triceratops's head, being careful not to frighten it. Then he reached down and gave Jamie a hand up. Soon they were both sitting on the leathery neck and holding onto one of the triceratops's horns.

"We're away from the huge legs, but what if it throws us off?" Jamie asked.

"I don't think it even noticed us," Tom replied.

Their triceratops finished its ginkgo fruit and then raised its head and began to follow the herd. Wanna stared up at them, his head to one side.

"Hey, Wanna." Tom waved. "Look at us!"

"This is awesome!" declared Jamie. "It's like being on the handlebars of a giant bike."

"Hold on tight for a bumpy ride," said Tom.

The dinosaur swayed as it plodded steadily through the tangle of jungle vines and trees. Jamie and Tom slid about, dodging the passing branches while Wanna trotted among the legs of the herd, grunting at the top of his voice.

"This is much faster than walking!" Jamie laughed.

Suddenly, the boys could see bright light through the giant leaves and branches. The herd left the jungle behind and lumbered out into the dazzling sunlight of the plains.

CHAPTER 4

Jamie squinted at the open land shimmering in the heat.

"Look!" He pointed. "There's the river again—it comes down from the mountains." He leaned his notebook on one of the triceratops's horns and drew a winding line from the mountain peaks across the plains to the jungle.

"In a way, we're the first people ever to make a map," said Tom, as the herd moved steadily across the sweltering plains.

"The first explorers riding out on safari," declared Jamie, laughing. "This is great. I can see for miles!"

"Look at all these fantastic dinosaurs," Tom said. He pointed to a slow-moving herd grazing on the leaves of some trees and spoke to an imaginary camera. "This is Tom Clay, reporting live from Dino World, on the Great Plains. Who needs a jeep when you have the luxury of T-Tops Travel?"

Jamie laughed. He knew Tom wanted to be a famous wildlife presenter one day.

Tom went on. "Here, we are watching the alamosaurs reaching their long necks to the highest branches, and farther in the distance we can see the strange dwellings that we are about to investigate. Stay tuned for what could be the most exciting discovery of all time!"

The T-Tops lumbered on as the boys watched the scenery go by.

"Can you see that weird rock there?" said Tom, checking his compass. "Over to the east."

"It looks like a huge fang," Jamie said. "Let's call it Fang Rock!" He drew in the pointy rock and labeled it. Then he looked up. "Hey, we're really close to the houses now." He hurriedly put his notebook away. "They're at least three times as tall as my dad!"

The thin towers stood in a silent group in the baking heat, silent and seemingly uninhabited.

"I don't think they are houses," said Jamie. The mounds were made out of bumpy orange dirt and had deep crevices running down them. There weren't any windows or doors, and Jamie couldn't imagine what kind of creature could live in them.

"This feels weird," said Tom.

"As if something's waiting to happen," Jamie whispered.

The herd stopped a little way from the strange towers and mooed anxiously.

"They're signaling again," said Tom. "They don't seem to like the towers, either."

"I don't think Wanna understands their language," Jamie said.

Instead of being cautious, Wanna was scrabbling excitedly at the bottom of one of the towers. All of a sudden, a stream of orange insects was pouring out of the hole and all over the little dinosaur. Wanna jumped back, batting at his face with his claws.

"Termites!" gasped Tom. "These are termite mounds."

The ant-like creatures were as big as mice. Jamie had never seen anything like them. Wanna was yelping and shaking himself as they crawled all over him.

"Wanna is too quick for them," said Jamie, as the little dinosaur did a frantic dance. "He's flinging them off with all that jerking around!"

37

"But he's scaring the triceratops!" Tom cried.

The triceratops stamped their feet in alarm and backed off, jostling one another. The shaking of the earth seemed to wake the termites, and thousands of them poured out of every mound. Jamie saw the bugs stream up the legs of the leader of the herd and into its eyes and nose.

The leader tossed its head like an angry bull to shake the insects off, but it was no use. It couldn't move as easily as small, agile Wanna. Suddenly, it bellowed in terror and charged straight through the termite city! Dry dirt and insects scattered everywhere.

Jamie and Tom felt their T-Tops lurching forward, as the other dinosaurs began to run.

"It's a stampede!" yelled Jamie. "Hold on!"

The boys clung to the horns as the herd took off through the cloud of orange dust. Jamie felt like a rodeo rider being bucked about. Then he felt a prickle on his leg and looked down to see a termite crawling on him. Despite the bumping,

Jamie managed to flick it away quickly. But soon, a whole army of termites was crawling over their T-Tops's head toward him.

Jamie tried to knock them away, but all the movement made his backpack slip from his shoulder! He flung out an arm to catch it as it fell, but it was too late. Jamie's backpack tumbled to the ground and disappeared beneath the cloud of dust.

Jamie couldn't believe it. He had lost his precious Fossil Finder and his notebook—and there was nothing he could do about it.

Insects were scuttling all over him now, crawling in his hair and down his neck.

"Yow!" Jamie wailed as one termite bit him on the leg. Pain shot right down to his foot.

"I've been bitten, too!" cried Tom.

The boys tried to ignore the horrible itching and just clung on for dear life.

"Where's Wanna?" yelled Tom.

"I don't know!" Jamie shouted. "I can't see him!"

The stampede rushed forward and all at once the herd plunged downward.

"We're going down the riverbank!" Tom leaned back and gripped tightly as they approached the water.

Jamie gulped. "And we're not stopping!"

CHAPTER 5

SPLASH!

Their triceratops plunged into the churning river. The boys were thrown into the water among the giant thrashing dinosaurs and drowning insects. Jamie swam up to the surface and held his hands out, keeping him away from the dinosaurs' bodies and horns.

The huge dinosaurs stood in the water, seemingly relieved that the biting termites were being swept away by the river.

"They wanted to wash the termites off," Jamie managed to splutter.

"And us, too!" Tom replied. The boys felt the pull of the river and soon were sucked into the current.

"Thanks for the ride!" Jamie called out as they left their triceratops taxi far behind.

Jamie heard a grunting noise nearby. "Wanna!" he cried. The little dinosaur was running along the riverbank, trying to keep pace with them and he had something in his mouth.

"Your backpack!" Tom exclaimed. "It's safe!"

"Go, Wanna!" shouted Jamie.

Jamie and Tom were both good swimmers but the current was too strong for them to swim to the edge. When a log swept by, Jamie and Tom grabbed on to its stubby branches.

"Phew," gasped Tom as he got a good hold. He checked out the river ahead. "Do you think there are any champsosaurs in here?"

"I hope not," Jamie groaned. "I think we've met enough prehistoric beasts for one day."

The boys' log floated into a patch of shadow and Tom looked up. "It's Fang Rock!" he said. "We must be going toward Ginkgo Hill—and home!"

"Maybe it will take us all the way back, and save us the walk." Jamie grinned.

The river twisted around Fang Rock and out into the sunshine again. They could see Wanna on the bank. He was jumping up and down and grunting excitedly.

48

"What's the matter with Wanna?" Tom wondered aloud.

Jamie heard the sound of rushing water, and soon the boys' log was being knocked this way and that between sharp rocks. The water churned and bubbled, and Jamie realized that he could see the river disappear ahead of them. The land on either side of the river fell away and Jamie realized what Wanna was trying to warn them about. "It's a waterfall!"

The boys kicked frantically toward the bank, but

the current was too strong. The log bumped and spun on toward the dangerous drop. Just before the boys were about to go over, the log suddenly caught between two rocks. The boys barely managed to hold on as white water crashed over their shoulders.

"Phew!" exclaimed Jamie. He could just see over the fall, down to a large swirling pool below and was relieved that the log had saved them. He gave Tom a wobbly smile. "Let's get out of here."

Creeeeak!

"What was that?" he gasped.

"The log's splitting from the force of the current!" yelled Tom. "We're going to go over the waterfall!"

Jamie grabbed his arm. "Take a deep breath when you fall!" he shouted urgently. "Start swimming the moment you can!"

Crack!

The log broke and the boys were sucked through the white foaming water and over the edge.

CHAPTER 6

"**A**aaah!" Jamie shouted as he plummeted down and down.

He took a huge breath just in time.

SPLASH!

Jamie hit the churning water and plunged under the surface, tumbling around and around. He felt the waterfall pushing him to the bottom of the river. He opened his eyes but it was murky and dark. All he could see were

bubbles swirling around him. He couldn't even tell which way was up.

Then his foot touched rock. He pushed away hard, kicking his legs for all they were worth. At last he was at the surface, gulping in the wonderful air. He swam around, looking for Tom. He hoped his friend was all right!

Suddenly, the water beside him erupted and Tom bobbed up like a cork, gasping for breath.

Jamie and Tom looked up in awe at the huge waterfall behind them. "We made it!"

"A huge waterfall, an army of termites, a ride on a triceratops," Tom said. "Another great adventure in Dino World!"

The boys swam away from the waterfall and let the gentle current take them downstream. Ahead, the river disappeared back into the jungle. The current swept them around to the right, where the trees were dense and tangled with vines.

The river now became wider and slower. With weak strokes, the boys made their way to the side and grabbed ahold of an overhanging branch.

"I can touch the bottom," gasped Tom. "There's a ledge."

They dragged themselves out of the water and collapsed on the safe, dry bank.

Grunk!

Grunk!

Wanna bounded up and threw himself on them, licking and nudging them in turn. Then he disappeared into the undergrowth and came back a moment later with the backpack in his mouth. He dropped it in front of the boys.

Jamie sat up. "He kept it safe! Good job, Wanna. You're a real friend."

Tom reached over and pulled a ginkgo fruit out of the bag. "You deserve this!" he said, giving it to Wanna. The little dinosaur gobbled it down and gave Tom another huge lick.

"Yuck!" he cried, pushing him away. "Stink-o breath!"

"Where are we?" asked Jamie.

"Well, you've got the map!" laughed Tom.

Jamie pulled it out and the boys had a look around. There was a steep slope ahead of them, covered in a thick wall of trees.

"I can just hear the

waterfall," said Tom. He got to his feet and peered through the binoculars. "Yes, it's back there. It must be—look, there's the point of Fang Rock." He checked his compass. "It's east of here."

They looked at their map.

"And the river comes from the mountains in the northeast and flows across the plains." Jamie traced it with his finger.

"Then it goes through the jungle here—where we are," added Tom.

Jamie gazed at the trees ahead of them. "Then we must be at the bottom of Ginkgo Hill. Told you it would save us the walk!"

Tom checked his watch. "Lucky this is waterproof," he grinned. "It's not long before the tide comes in. We don't want to get trapped in the cliffs."

Jamie nodded. "Grandpa will be back with his lobsters and he'll be wondering where we are." He picked up his backpack. "Who'd have thought making a map would be such an adventure?"

They climbed back up Ginkgo Hill. As they passed the break in the trees, Jamie looked back out over the plains. He could see the termite mounds in the distance, and beyond that, on the other side of the river, was the grazing triceratops herd.

"Those termite bites really hurt when we got them," said Jamie, pulling up his trousers to reveal a purple bump the size of an apricot. "But they don't really hurt anymore."

"Ew!" Tom crinkled up his nose. "That looks so gross." Tom pulled up his T-shirt to reveal a bite on his stomach that had a greenish ring around it.

"Yours is even bigger!" Jamie declared.

"Prehistoric bug bites." Tom poked the squishy bump which seemed ready to pop at any minute. "We'd better not let anyone see these! We'd never be able to explain them."

Wanna bounded along with them, but as they reached the entrance to the cave, he slowed down and lowered his head.

Grunk?

"See you, Wanna," said Jamie, patting him on his hard, flat head. "We'll be back soon."

 61

"And that's a promise!" added Tom. He pulled out the last two ginkgo fruits.

Wanna wagged his tail and gobbled up his treat happily.

Jamie and Tom stepped into the cave. Jamie placed his feet in the dinosaur footprints and felt the ground get harder as he went. On his fifth step, he was plunged into inky darkness, back in the cave in Dinosaur Cove. A moment later, Tom was standing next to him.

Jamie flicked on his flashlight and led the way out of the cave, down the rock fall, and back along the path to the beach.

"What an adventure!" said Tom.

"Better than any theme park," agreed Jamie. He fished out his notebook and flicked to the map. "Look how far we traveled today! Right out on to the plain—and back the quick way!" He pointed to Fang Rock. "The waterfall was just here. What should we call it?"

"Crashing Rock Falls!" declared Tom.

"Cool! Maybe I'll draw us going over the edge." Jamie grinned.

"Ahoy there, boys!" Jamie's grandfather was rowing back toward the beach.

The boys waved and ran down to the sea.

"Come on," he called. "I can't land the boat without your help."

Jamie and Tom jumped into the surf and waded out to the boat, helping him pull the boat up the beach.

"The moment we're done, Jamie," he said as they unloaded the full lobster pots, "you must show Tom the new triceratops skull. It's sixty-five million years old." He clapped Tom on the back. "I bet you haven't seen anything like that before!"

Jamie and Tom smiled at each other. Jamie's grandfather would never believe what they *had* seen today in Dino World!

Far Away Mountains

Crashing Rock Falls

Great Plains

Fang Rock

Ginkgo Hill

GLOSSARY

Alamosaurus – a gigantic dinosaur with a vegetarian diet that searched for food with its long neck and tiny head while protecting itself with its long, whip-like tail.

Champsosaurus – crocodile-like prehistoric creature with a long, thin, tooth-filled snout, living and hunting in rivers and swamps.

Fossil – the remains or imprint of plants or animals found in rocks. They help scientists unravel the mysteries of prehistoric times.

Ginkgo – a tree native to China called a "living fossil" because fossils of it have been found dating back millions of years, yet they are still around today. Also known as the stink-bomb tree because of its smelly apricot-like fruit.

Herbivore – an animal that only eats plants; a vegetarian.

Termite – ant-like insects that grow as big as mice in Dino World. These prehistoric pests lived and worked together to build orange house-high mounds out of soil and spit, and there are still several kinds of termites around today.

Triceratops (T-Tops) – a three-horned, plant-eating dinosaur which looks like a rhinoceros.

Tyrannosaurus Rex (T-Rex) – a meat-eating dinosaur with a huge tail, two strong legs, but two tiny arms. T-Rex was one of the biggest and scariest dinosaurs.

Wannanosaurus – a dinosaur that only ate plants and used its hard, flat skull to defend itself. Named after the place it was discovered: Wannano in China.

T-REX TROUBLE SUPERSIZED!!!

A hunt for fossils leads Tom and Jamie to the entrance of a prehistoric world—and face-to-face with T-Rex. Will this gigantic carnivore see them as his next meal—or will the boys make it out alive?